Countries We Come From

Indonesia

by Rachel Rose

Consultant: Marjorie Faulstich Orellana, PhD
Professor of Urban Schooling
University of California, Los Angeles

BEARPORT PUBLISHING
New York, New York

Credits

Cover, © nortongo/Shutterstock and © ErmakovaElena/iStock; TOC, © Natthakan Jommanee/EyeEm/Getty Images; 4, © Guitar photographer/Shutterstock; 5T, © Sirisak_baokaew/Shutterstock; 5B, © Rostislav Ageev/Shutterstock; 7, © Shann Biglione/Getty Images; 8–9, © Ramses/Getty Images; 9T, © Antoine Boureau/Getty Images; 10, © Konstantin Aksenov/Shutterstock; 11, © Afriandi/Getty Images; 12, © Anton Petrus/Getty Images; 13T, © ANDREYGUDKOV/Getty Images; 13B, © Jolanda Aalbers/Shutterstock; 14, © Huy Thoai/Shutterstock; 15T, © kellymarken/Getty Images; 15B, © Rhododendrites/Wikimedia; 16T, © David Evison/Shutterstock; 16B, © Photo Dharma/Wikimedia; 17, © Unknown/Wikimedia; 18T, © INDONESIAPIX/Shutterstock; 18B, © Adwo/Shutterstock; 19, © Andre Soriton/Shutterstock; 20, © Tropical studio/Shutterstock; 20–21, © Didier Marti/Getty Images; 22, © em faies/Shutterstock; 23T, © paul prescott/Shutterstock; 23B, © alfin tofler/Shutterstock; 24T, © Janet Faye Hastings/Shutterstock; 24B, © taveesak srisomthavil/Shutterstock; 25, © Photographer Nick Measures/Getty Images; 26, © NicolasMcComber/Getty Images; 27, © SantiPhotoSS/Shutterstock; 28, © CHEN WS/Shutterstock; 29T, © Sergiy Kuzmin/Shutterstock; 29B, © zahirul alwan/Shutterstock; 30M, © tanukiphoto/Getty Images; 30B, © Sergiy Borakovskyy/EyeEm/Getty Images; 31 (T to B), © Andreas H/Shutterstock, © Pichayanon Watjanasoontorn/EyeEm/Getty Images, © Frans Mendur/Wikimedia, © David Evison/Shutterstock, © skeeze/Pixabay, and © mTaira/Shutterstock; 32, © raclro/Getty Images.

Publisher: Kenn Goin
Senior Editor: Joyce Tavolacci
Creative Director: Spencer Brinker
Design: Debrah Kaiser
Photo Researcher: Book Buddy Media

Library of Congress Cataloging-in-Publication Data

Names: Rose, Rachel, 1968– author.
Title: Indonesia / by Rachel Rose.
Description: New York, New York: Bearport Publishing Company, Inc., 2020. | Series: Countries we come from | Includes bibliographical references and index.
Identifiers: LCCN 2019014396 (print) | LCCN 2019015027 (ebook) | ISBN 9781642805796 (ebook) | ISBN 9781642805253 (library)
Subjects: LCSH: Indonesia—Juvenile literature.
Classification: LCC DS615 (ebook) | LCC DS615 .R67 2019 (print) | DDC 959.8—dc23
LC record available at https://lccn.loc.gov/2019014396

For more information, write to Bearport Publishing Company, Inc., 45 West 21st Street, Suite 3B, New York, New York 10010. Printed in the United States of America.

10 9 8 7 6 5 4 3 2 1

Contents

This Is Indonesia

Beautiful

Full of Life

Wild

Indonesia is the largest country in Southeast Asia.

About 263 million people live there!

Indonesia is made up of more than 17,500 islands!

Many of Indonesia's islands were created by volcanoes.

The volcanoes rise high above the land.

Sometimes, they still **erupt**!

Indonesia's Lake Toba was formed at the top of a volcano. It's the biggest volcanic lake in the world.

Indonesia has thousands of miles of beaches.

Lush forests cover about half of the country.

Sometimes, earthquakes strike Indonesia. They can cause deadly **tsunamis** that flood the land.

There's wonderful wildlife in Indonesia.

Orangutans swing from the trees.

The one-horned Javan rhinoceros looks for plants to eat.

The Komodo dragon is the largest lizard in the world! It has lived in Indonesia for millions of years.

There are over 40,000 kinds of plants in Indonesia.
Colorful orchids grow there.

The pitcher plant catches insects in its rounded leaves!

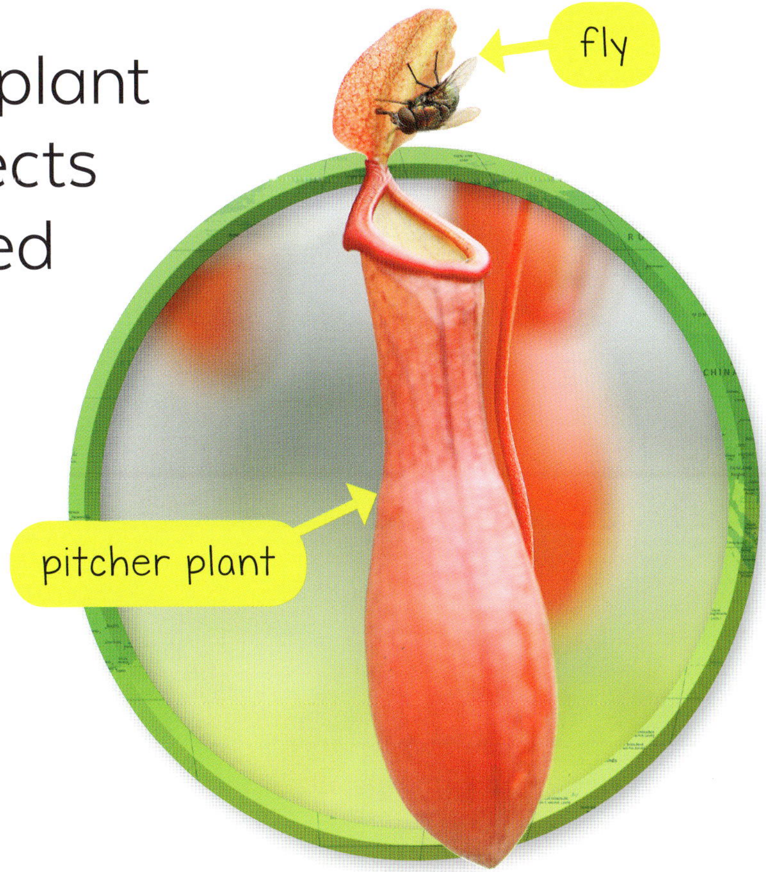

Indonesia's corpse plant has the world's largest flower. It smells like a dead animal!

Indonesia has a long history.

Native people have lived there for thousands of years.

a Dani tribesman

Some groups built boats and sailed the seas.

Europeans arrived in the 1500s.

They were harsh rulers and controlled the islands for many years.

Indonesia finally became **independent** in 1945.

Religion is important to Indonesians.

Most people are Muslim.

Other people are Hindu, Buddhist, or Christian.

Muslim worshippers

There are many beautiful Hindu temples on the island of Bali.

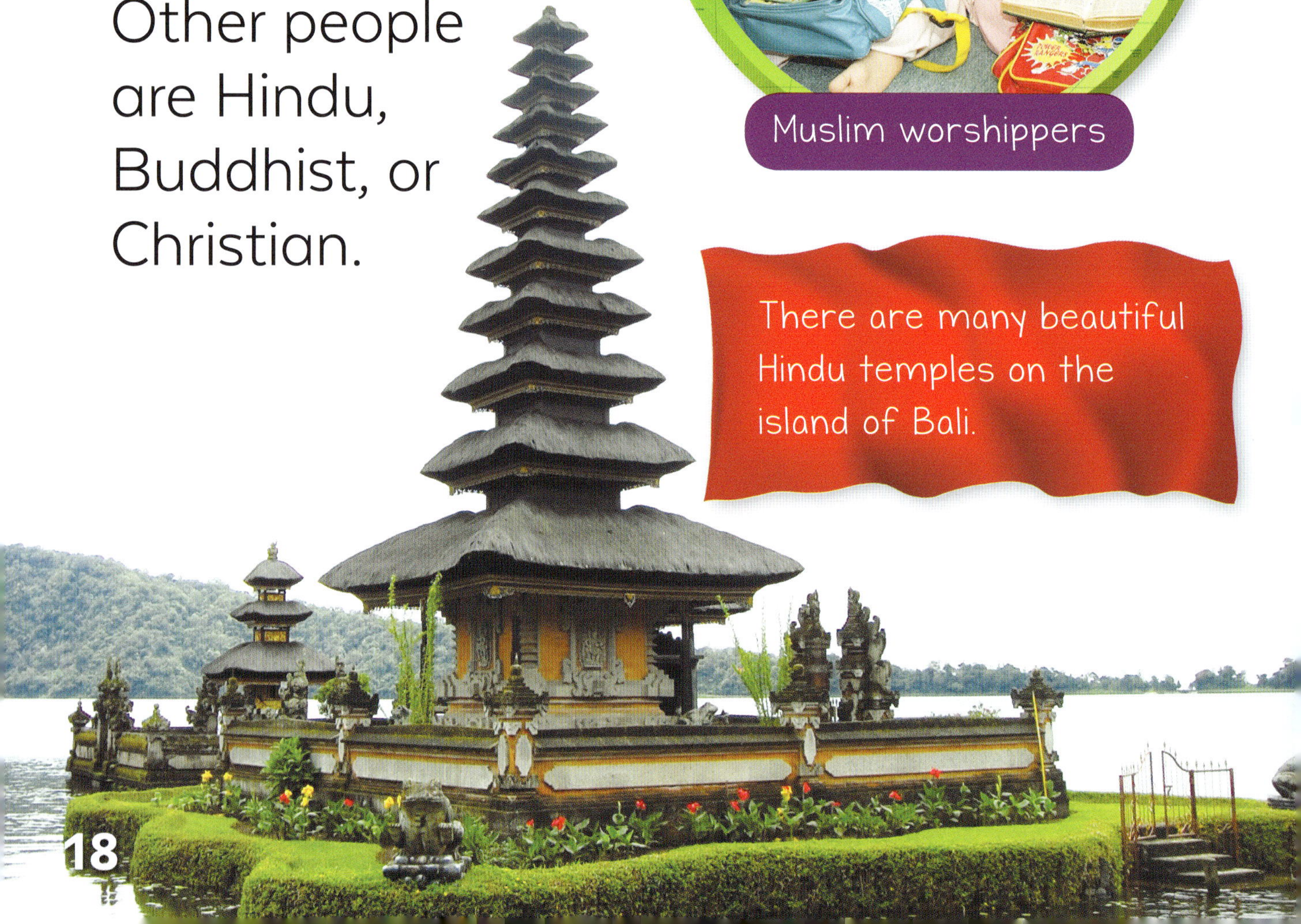

a church in Luwuk, Indonesia

Jakarta is Indonesia's **capital** and largest city.

It sits on the island of Java.

Almost half of Indonesia's population lives on Java.

Puppet shows are very popular in Indonesia. Jakarta has its very own puppet museum!

More than ten million people live in Jakarta.

Outside of cities, most Indonesians work as farmers.

Many people grow rice in wet fields.

Some farmers live in houses on stilts.

The stilts keep the houses from flooding.

house on stilts

Farmers also grow tea on big farms called plantations.

Rice is a very popular food in Indonesia.

It's served with meat, fish, and vegetables.

durian fruit

Durian cake is a favorite dessert. Durian is a creamy, prickly fruit. It tastes good but smells like dirty socks!

Indonesians often eat with their fingers.

Hundreds of different languages are spoken in Indonesia.

Bahasa (bah-HAH-sah) Indonesia is the main language.

This is how you say *thank you* in Bahasa Indonesia:

Terima kasih
(TEH-ree-muh KAH-see)

This is how you say *you're welcome:*

Sama-sama
(SAH-muh SAH-muh)

Most Indonesians speak Bahasa Indonesia as their second language.

Badminton is one of Indonesia's most popular sports.

It's played with rackets and a **shuttlecock**.

Indonesians are some of the best badminton players in the world!

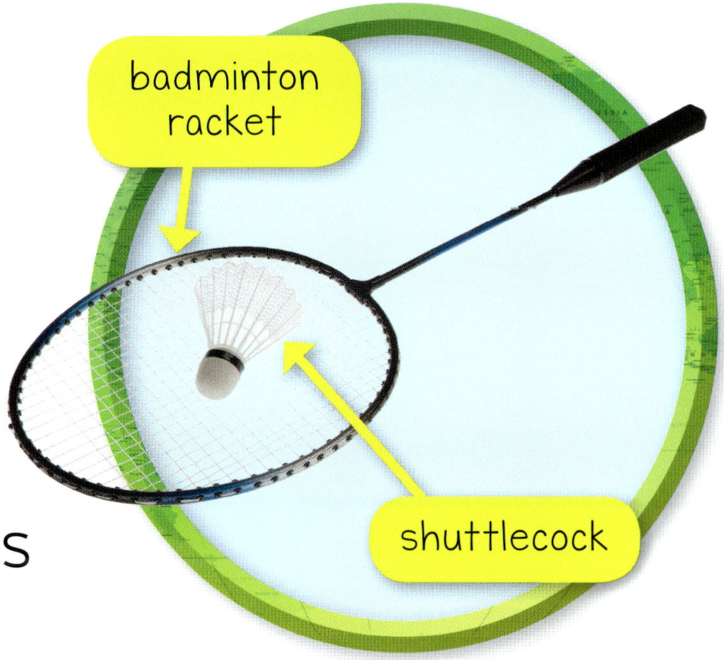

Flying kites is also a favorite Indonesian pastime.

Fast Facts

Capital city: Jakarta

Population of Indonesia: About 263 million

Main language: Bahasa Indonesia

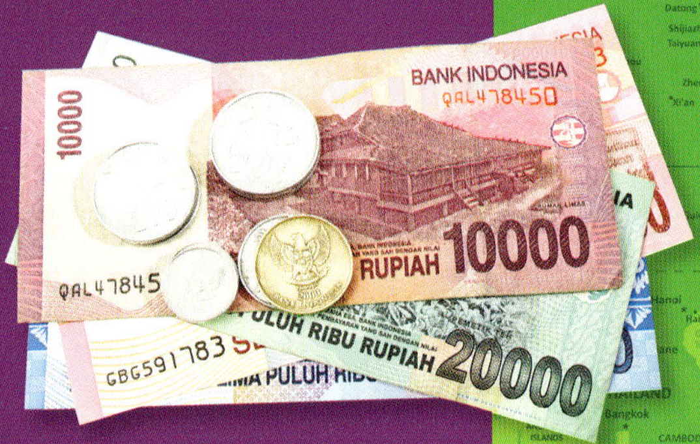

Money: Indonesian rupiah

Major religion: Islam

Neighboring countries: East Timor, Malaysia, and Papua New Guinea

Cool Fact: Indonesians call their country *Tanah Air Kita*. It means "Our Land and Water."

Glossary

capital (KAP-uh-tuhl) the city where a country's government is based

erupt (ee-RUPT) when a volcano explodes, sending out ash, rocks, and lava

independent (in-duh-PEN-duhnt) free from outside control

native (NAY-tiv) belonging to a particular place

shuttlecock (SHUH-tul-kahk) a small cone-shaped object that is hit over a net in badminton

tsunamis (tsoo-NAH-meez) huge waves caused by an underwater earthquake or volcano

Index

Read More

Lim, Robin. *Indonesia (Country Explorers).* Minneapolis, MN: Lerner (2010).

Owings, Lisa. *Indonesia (Exploring Countries).* Minneapolis, MN: Bellwether (2013).

Learn More Online

To learn more about Indonesia, visit
www.bearportpublishing.com/CountriesWeComeFrom

About the Author

Rachel Rose lives in San Francisco. She loves visiting new countries and is hoping to add Indonesia to her list of places to go.